TALL TALES
from a RANCH

TALL TALES
from a RANCH

by ANNIE M. BOYCE

Illustrated by Walter A. McKinney

The Naylor Company

These Tall Tales From A Ranch are lovingly dedicated to my father, Robert Allen Boyce, and my uncles, Charles Henry Boyce, William Ward Boyce, A. James Boyce and Johnnie Boyce who drove up the Old Chisholm Trail many times.

Foreword

I was born in the Southwest, and have lived here all my life. I am a native Texan. I lived on a ranch and a farm until I was fourteen years old. My parents took me and my five sisters to the small town of Runge, Texas, eight miles from my home, where I went to school with four of my sisters until I graduated from high school.

Then my parents sent me to the Southwest Texas State Teacher's College at San Marcos, Texas, where I graduated and received a B. A. degree, and became a teacher in the public schools of Texas. My four sisters received the same training, earned degrees, and also became teachers in the public schools of Texas.

Later, I and my sisters went back to the same college and received our M.A. degrees. The name of my thesis is *A Red Man's Foster Son*. It is the story of General Sam Houston's life and leadership in the Battle of San Jacinto, which won the freedom of Texas. This thesis is written on the fourth grade level. My maternal grandmother's name, before her marriage, was Sarah Jane (Kitty) Houston. Her father, Robert Houston, and Gen. Sam were first cousins.

I am a public school teacher in the San Antonio Independent School District. I teach the second grade. I have been teaching here for more than twenty-five years.

My father, who graduated from Baylor University in Waco, went up the Old Chisholm Trail the first time at the ripe age of fourteen, with his two older brothers. They drove their own herds of longhorn cattle. His brothers had traveled the Old Chisholm Trail many times before.

When I was a child, my father highly entertained my sisters and me with stories about his adventures up The Trail. The mood was upon him most often early in the morning, when he churned for mother while she was getting breakfast. He greatly magnified objects and instances in most of his adventures.

Being inspired by my father's stories, I have written eighteen tall tales for my own fun and enjoyment. These stories tell about what happened on a ranch and in its immediate vicinity in the West and Southwest. The events and objects on this ranch are, perhaps, somewhat magnified; the reader will understand.

Introduction
THE BRUCE RANCH

"BILLIE, BILLIE, it's time to get up," called out Aunt Sue from the kitchen.

It was now five o-clock in the morning. All the people on this ranch arose early. In fact, the Bruce Ranch was

similar to any other ranch except for the miraculous things which occurred in the tales that follow.

Now Aunt Sue liked to get up each morning at four o-clock, and drink her coffee while she listened to Old Pancho, the big steer, chew his cud. "Billie," as she called her husband, liked to sleep until five, and he never took coffee. He always drank buttermilk, mixed with clabber and cream, for his breakfast. These two kind old people, owners and operators of the Bruce Ranch, lived in a large one and one-half story house, built by them in their younger days. The house had once been handsomely decorated inside, and painted white with green trimmings on the outside, but it needed a new coat of paint — to say nothing of new paper.

"The Big White House," as some of the hands called it, was built on the highest hill in the country, about midway on the northern border of the ranch. Below it, as far as the eye could see, tenant houses and windmills dotted the landscape. In the pasture lands, such shrubs as catclaw, ebony, mesquite, prickly pear, gran-jenu, and oak filled in the landscape.

The ranch, which was almost rectangular in shape, extended ten miles in length, and four miles in width. A public road cut through the length of it on one side, while a railroad ran along the other boundary. A small creek, called Frog Gully, flowed across the southeast corner.

Aunt Sue and Uncle Billie, as they were lovingly called because of their many nieces and nephews, were known for miles around. Moreover, they had given financial aid to many friends in their community, not counting that given to a great host of relatives.

Uncle Billie had driven his own cattile up The Trail eighteen times. Also, he had acquired a B. A. degree from Concrete College, now extinct, and had taught mathematics and English in the same college for a number of years.

Finally, in his later bachelorhood, he had won the heart of "Sue," who became his wife. They had never had children of their own, but some relatives or friends were always visiting them.

Contents

Old Pancho

OLD PANCHO was an old steer who roamed
the range before fences were built. He
was a monstrous beast, belonging now to the
Bruce Ranch. Each summer he made his
bed down by the yard fence of the
ranch house on the south side, and his
breath caused the breeze to be
warm and muggy. When he chewed

his cud at night, his horns tapped on the roof of the ranch house. Really, Uncle Billie and Aunt Sue were so used to the rhythmic tapping that they could not go to sleep at night unless they heard it. Aunt Sue confided to one of the neighbors that this was the reason she and "Billie" never spent the night away from home.

Just as regular as the years came, they sent a carpenter up on the roof to repair the places where Old Pancho had worn holes in the shingles with his horns.

Now, the cattle flies that particular season were more annoying than usual. One night, this old steer started hooking at them after he had bedded down. When he jerked his head from side to side, his horns were so large and so long that he knocked all the lightning rods off one end of the second story. Of course, the carpenters had to replace these rods, too.

Furthermore, Old Pancho's horns were something to remember. Alberto Monte, a half-Indian workman, was one person who would never forget them. "Monte," as he was called by Uncle Billie, was coming to the house one day to be advised on some agrarian problem. This half-breed, who was more Indian than Mexican, had about twelve whiskers hanging from his chin; but he was so proud of them that he never shaved. Moreover, he loved very bright colors and always wore red, green, or yellow shirts.

That day he had on a bright red shirt. Old Pancho was standing by a tree near the house. When he saw Monte's shirt, he was curious to see what it was. So he started toward this half-breed Indian. Monte wondered how he would get past Old Pancho to the house. Old Pancho never had molested anyone before, but Monte was very fearful by now. He thought he might dodge Old Pancho and run behind a tree, then make his way to the house. Old Pancho was clever too, and seemed determined to inspect the red shirt. With his head hanging low, he gave a loud bellow, and ran toward Monte, beating him to the tree.

However, one of his horns caught on the roots of a giant oak while the other caught behind the tree, no less than fifty feet away, where Monte wanted to hide. They were locked fast for a time. Before long, however, the roots began to pop and the ground to crack. Monte ran under the horns to make his getaway, but the sun was shining so brightly that the reflection of the sun on Old Pancho's horns caused Monte's beard to catch on fire, and burn completely off. Some people in that part of the country declared that the same thing caused many grass fires there later. After that, Old Pancho had to have a pasture to himself — for another reason, though.

It had rained hard, very hard, for about twelve hours one night in the spring. Old Pancho, not liking the weather, got up from his bed and walked about, all over the pasture. Uncle Billie had as many as six hundred sheep in that pasture. The next morning when he went to the barn, as usual, to do a few chores, he was amazed to see so many of his sheep missing.

He saddled Old Baby, his old cow horse, and started out to hunt for them. He had not gone very far when Old Baby suddenly stopped. He was on the brink of something. Uncle Billie rode nearer and peeped cautiously over it. It was one of Old Pancho's tracks, no less than forty feet deep, and twenty or thirty of the sheep had fallen into it. Down there on the bottom, they were just roving around in the mud and water. All over the pasture, each track had no less than twenty sheep in it. Blocks and tackles did yeoman's duty for nearly two days getting them out.

One sunshiny day while Old Pancho was grazing casually in his new pasture, an icy norther suddenly blew up. His shadow froze to the ground, and when it thawed out the next week, it caused cloudy weather all over the Southwest for more than three weeks.

Grandpap Rattler

AFTER THE DRAW between the rat and Grandpap Rattler, or Old Lucifer, as some of the natives called him, Uncle Billie decided he would stay clear of that part of the pasture for awhile. One of his renters, Herk Lunkins, swore that while he was repairing the fence near the cave, he found small rattlers in holes about every two feet for a mile and a half around this cave. When one snake rattled, it shook the ground and every rattler then would raise its head from its hole to see what was happening. All of them were descendants of Grandpap Rattler. Furthermore, Herk Lunkins said Uncle Billie was lucky not to have had a collision with some of them the day he and Old Baby chased the big rat in that part of the country.

The farmers for miles around threatened to set a watch for old Grandpap Rattler, so that when he crawled out of his neighborhood, they could catch him. They just never did, though.

One day when Herk Lunkins was out rounding up the cattle during branding season, he saw something that made him scratch his head and blink his eyes a couple of times. Grandpap Rattler was about four miles from his den. He had swallowed five head of goats, and Uncle Billie's finest Brahma bull.

Moreover, about this time, Grandpap Rattler was getting pretty sick at his stomach. The five goats which were swallowed first had teamed up on the Brahma bull inside the rattler, and were giving him some rare hornings. The bull, however, could not move very much, because the snake had swallowed all of him but his horns, and these were acting as props, holding the snake's mouth wide open.

Furthermore, the goats nibbled and horned on Grandpap Rattler's insides too; but not liking the smell, they calmly walked out at his mouth again. Ab Jones, Jr., one of the ranch boys, declared he had never seen "such doings."

But to get back to the story: Herk hurried back to the house to get some help to kill the snake. On the way, he met Hank Muldon, Ab Jones, Jr., and a few other neighbors. Ab, hurrying off to the snake, said he knew the rattler must be wandering somewhere in "these parts" because, a few days ago, he had missed two head of his finest horses. In fact, they were his carriage horses. He had hunted for them for two days before he found them, lost in Grandpap Rattler's freshly shed skin. The skin was stretched along about four miles of his hog-wire fence, and the hogs were climbing up on the skin under some of the tallest pecan trees, and were eating the green nuts. Some of his hogs were sick right then from eating too many of them.

Now, when the neighbors had gotten back to the old snake, he was feeling better. He had finished swallowing the bull, and had raised himself up a hundred and fifty feet in the air, and was watching from all directions. His tail was buzzing so that he had slung his rattles over the country within a sixteen mile circumference. The people in that particular section of the country went underground in their storm houses for two whole days, because they thought they were being showered with meteors.

Grandpap Rattler knew when he was cornered, but he was going to put up a stiff fight. He was now poised to strike. He struck at Hank Muldon, but Hank dodged him and fell safely under a cactus bush. Grandpap Rattler, being nearly blind from a previous fight, over-leaped his mark four miles or more and fell into a landing field. His head, however, struck a sawmill in an adjoining pasture and the big saws did the trick. His head was severed clear of his body! The Brahma bull, with only a few scratches and sanguinary intentions, came forth quickly from the snake and ran away, bellowing, into the woods.

Meantime, the snake's head, as is the case with many snake heads, backed off through the woods and struck a railroad siding where a caboose was stationed. It knocked the caboose off the tracks and tore up the rails for a hundred yards or more. The head then moved on over the caboose into a field and settled itself to die. The mouth opened and the fangs stood straight up in the air. In a few moments, the poison started bubbling up from them like water from an artesian well. The County Health Department came out and condemned the field, and put up a big danger sign saying, "POISON FIELD." For ten years this field lay fallow.

Where the head was severed from the body, the snake meat was white like fish. Herk Lunkins said it looked just like fish steak, and took a cut of it home for dinner. Some of the other neighbors did likewise. They reported favorably on this new-found meat, and that was the beginning of rattlesnake sandwiches. To this day, they are served in the most fashionable cafes all over the Southwest. Some people think they are a great delicacy.

Grandpap Rattler's meat disappeared quickly. Each person told his neighbor how delicious it was, until nothing but the rattler's skeleton was left on the landing field. Finally, the government put a cover over it and used it for airplane hangars.

One fine morning, Uncle Billie decided to go across the road into his other pasture to inspect some dogies. He saddled Old Baby, his cattle horse, now almost retired from service, and started out.

As they were going through a thicket of catclaw and gran-jenu, Old Baby galloped toward what he thought was a cow. Now, there was one characteristic about this old cattle horse, likable or not: when he saw a head of cattle he was determined to round it up. Therefore, in spite of all Uncle Billie's persuasion and guidance, Old Baby persisted in bringing in the cow. This cow had the longest, most peculiar tail imaginable. It was absolutely devoid of hair. The strange beast started running as fast as a streak of lightning. Old Baby tried to keep up with it, but he made little headway. Uncle Billie could not see much of it for the bushes and shrubs. However, he got a glimpse of it as it ran into a cave near the road. It was not a cow. It was a gigantic wood rat!

Finally, Uncle Billie, with his clothing half torn off, and Old Baby in a big lather, arrived at the mouth of the cave. Inside, a terrific chorus of shrieks was mingled with ear-splitting rattles. This was the home of Grandpap Rattler, the giant old rattlesnake. No one had found his den up to this time, but the hunters all over the country had been looking diligently for it.

Furthermore, the shrieks and rattles continued, and the rat fur began to fly. It made such a fog along the road for four or five miles that the State Highway Department put up a sign saying, "DANGER, DETOUR." Moreover, the Aviation Department even threatened to put up a beacon there to warn airplanes to fly upward of no less than ten miles high to get out of the dust and fur fog.

It was said that the fight was a draw between the rattler and the rat; that the rat came out with a battered nose, a couple of teeth knocked out, and his tail a trifle shorter. The rattler, it was discovered later, had an eye punctured, his nose gashed, and a part of his left fang broken off. Also, some of his scales — as large as auto cushions — were found in another pasture several miles away from his den.

A Prize Turkey

ONE FALL, Aunt Sue and Uncle Billie went to a Turkey Trot, known as a Fair in other places. There were prize turkeys on display from all over the Southwest. Aunt Sue decided then and there to buy a pair of those turkeys. Old Aunt Emma, her colored cook, would help her raise

them. A fat turkey was always good food right about Christmastime, and besides, Aunt Sue always gave a New Year's dinner for all the cow hands. She would need some turkeys.

The very next spring, Old Priss, as the turkey hen was called, stole her nest off in a pasture two miles away. Nevertheless, Uncle Jake, Aunt Emma's husband, found the nest one morning when he went to get the calves to do the milking. He came back to the house, and hooked two pair of mules to an old slide that had been used in hauling water before the windmills were built. He told Aunt Emma that he had found a turkey nest, and was going back to it.

Now Aunt Emma thought that Uncle Jake's mind was wandering again, since he had had a second attack of arthritis, but, good-humoredly, she watched him drive the mules and slide away. However, she sent little Moses, her favorite nephew, scouting through the bushes to watch Uncle Jake in case he acted queerer; then Moses was to come back and tell her what was happening. Aunt Sue told her that she should never have let Uncle Jake go on such a jaunt; that he had probably lost his mind completely. Moreover, Aunt Sue even threatened to send Herk Lunkins to take over the teams, but she never did.

Four hours later, here came Uncle Jake and little Moses bringing in the prize of the season, a great turkey egg. The freckles on that turkey egg were as big as dinner plates.

While the egg was being brought to the house, though, there was an accident that almost became a calamity. They were passing by the pigpen when the slide ran over a place in the road where the little pigs had been rooting. The egg rolled off the slide, struck a rock, broke open, and flooded the whole pigsty. The old mother pig and the little pigs had to swim around in the pen for two hours. Little Moses was carried along in the flood of egg, when, luckily, he caught on to the top rail of the sty. The roar from the flood was tremendous. Meanwhile, Uncle Jake was wading up to his neck in egg trying to unhook the teams, which were on the verge of stampeding. Immediately afterwards, little Moses, who had been screaming and clinging to the pen all the while, had to be rescued.

After the flood had receded somewhat, the ducks came out and had a good time swimming. The sun shone down very hot during that time, the egg dried, and all the ducks were glued hard and fast to the ground. There never was such a quacking noise. Aunt Emma rescued every duck. But when she pulled them out of this dried mixture of egg and mud, they were completely "de-feathered." Aunt Emma was very busy that fall knitting sweaters for all the ducks, as winter was just around the corner.

Pink Eyes

ONE NIGHT in mid-summer, just after a torrential rain had fallen, Uncle Jake, the old colored man, started to the calf pen, as usual, to let out the calves. As he stepped off the porch into the darkness, he stumbled over something.

"Git out fum hyeah, you hawgs!" he shouted.

But there was no movement at all.

"Mr. Lund all time a lettin' his hawgs out at dark," he said, half-talking to himself.

But when his eyes became more accustomed to the darkness, he looked about and saw hundreds of pink eyes, large and small, centered on him.

"Emme! Emme! De debbil's eyes am done gone pink! Bring me dat flash lamp and mah razor! Sumpin' gwine happen out hyeah!" he called loudly to his wife.

He turned the flashlight on, only to find hundreds of mosquitoes roving around the yard. They were ready now to attack him. He threw the flashlight into a group of the largest ones, and while they were fighting among themselves, he made his way back into the house by hiding behind this one's leg, that one's bill, and under the other one's wing. He cut two of them with his razor, and there was such a rush of blood that he had to wade through it up to his knees.

There never was a bigger fight nor a louder chorus of singing, fluttering, and whirring of wings. It sounded like a group of bombers fighting a few feet up in the air. Aunt Emma was afraid that the wind made by the whirring of their wings might blow down the house. The noise could be heard for two miles. Some people who were aroused from their peaceful slumbers thought that a neighborhood radio station was broadcasting some foolishness again about Mars or some other planet, and had gone haywire. Others thought that a cyclone might have struck somewhere in the vicinity.

The next morning, Uncle Jake and Aunt Emma had plenty of work to do. Aunt Emma had to clean mud a foot thick or more from her front porch, where these mosquitoes had tracked it in and out. Also, the yard was a regular bog hole. Furthermore, Uncle Jake was busy for a week loading wings, legs, bills, and bodies of dead mosquitoes on the old slide, and hauling them away to be burned. However, there were some leg bones left from the smaller mosquitoes that lay about the yard for weeks until two old wolf hounds, Rip and Filly, carried them away.

Uncle Jake thought the blood on the yard from the fight might create sickness; so he dug ditches which drained most of it off, while the sun dried up the remainder. Aunt Emma planted old-fashioned sunflower seed along the ditches, and the plants produced sunflowers as large around as wash tubs. The seeds from these flowers were as huge as the fruit from her pear trees.

On Frog Gully

(A GHOST STORY)

FROG GULLY was one place no one ever visited after sundown; at least, none of the colored folk. Hundreds of ghost stories had been told about this place.

Frog Gully was only a little creek that ran across the southeastern corner of the Bruce Ranch. Large perch could be caught there most any time. Great willow trees scattered their cool shade along the banks in the summertime. This made heavenly fishing for the colored ranch hands on drowsy spring or hot summer days.

Many hair-raising stories had been told among the colored workmen about Frog Gully. Some colored person would go fishing and fall asleep over his hook and line only to awaken after dark. This was the time ghosts always appeared! Now, Aunt Stella Johnson had had that experience. She told this story:

"I was a sittin' fishin' an' I was so tired dat I fall 'sleep. All of a sudden, I heerd the loudes' laughin', an' I open mah eyes. But I shet dem close tight ag'in quick! Dey wuz a big blue dappled hoss a-standin' by mah side, an' he wuz so big dat his haid done retched up in de clouds. I prayed to de Lawd an' I jump up. When I open mah eyes, dat hoss had done turn red as fiah, an' had jump dat gully an' wuz a-movin' ober de hill a-goin' lak lightnin' an' a wavin' his fiery tail. I got home somehow, but Lawsy, I don' remember."

Then there was the story about a big red eye appearing among the treetops, accompanied by an unearthly yell; and then disappearing suddenly.

Uncle Jake, the colored cook's husband, said he was out late one evening on Frog Gully — "an de Lawd he'p him nevah to be out dat late ag'in," — when he saw what looked like an old mule; but the more he looked at it, the stranger it became. It walked out of its skin and left it hanging in the air. Then the meat fell off the bones, leaving only the skeleton standing. Its skull became as large as a covered wagon; its teeth were green; and its eye sockets had a strange blue light in them. It made a deafening braying noise. Then the skull left the other part of the skeleton, and slid along the creek bank as if it were hunting for something.

Meantime, the part left standing was quivering, shaking,

and writhing all in one place. Soon, the meat came back to the bones; the hide flew back on the skeleton; it picked up its head; and galloped off through the dark bushes.

But the most gruesome and scary of all ghost stories was the one told by Slim Washington, a tall, hungry-looking colored man, who was known as a vagrant among his own people. His hair was long, his hat was torn, and his clothes were always ragged and dirty. Aunt Jenny Stokes (colored) once commented on Slim's clothes by saying they hung on him like a cotton sack on a broom handle. Moreover, she said he was "the no 'countes' niggah in de country"; and that she "knowed he done stole her fines' Plymouth Rock pullets, 'cause he come to her house de very nex' mawnin' after dey wuz stole, wid some of de feathers still a-hangin' to his ole coat. On top o' all dat, dis triflin' no 'count houn' tried to ax me fuh my daughter, Lizzie. An' dat wuz mo' gall den de United States hab debts an' strikes, an' dat be a few."

Anyway, one hot afternoon not far from the creek, Slim Washington had fallen asleep under a cool, shady oak tree. He said he was dreaming about a supper the colored folks were going to have down at their church. At this moment, he heard someone whispering very loud. When they tapped him on the shoulder, he awoke completely! He slightly but slyly opened one eye and peeped. What a sight he saw! There was a skull in mid-air with a big red eye blinking in it! It rolled back and forth and winked at him!

The next time he opened his eye, a man stood some distance away from him. The man was moaning and groaning. His throat was cut from ear to ear, and the blood was streaming down to the ground. Furthermore, his eyes seemed to bother him greatly. They kept falling out of his head and rolling on the ground toward Slim. The man kept picking up his eyes and putting them back in place.

About this time, Slim was having eye trouble, too! His eyes were rolling back and forth, searching for a chance to escape. Too, the man kept talking in a language absolutely unknown to this very frightened Negro. Soon, the ghost's arms fell off, and rolled down to the water's edge. His legs came off at his knees and rolled toward Slim, who by this time was backing away trying to get a tree between himself and the ghost. But in spite of all Slim could do, the man kept clear of all trees and came closer to him. Suddenly, this apparition breathed very loud and his heart popped out. Then his arms, hands, and limbs came back to his torso. He took his heart in one hand and threw it at Slim. The heart burst at the Negro's feet, yet there was no sign of its being on the ground. Slim almost fainted!

The specter then rose into the air ten or twelve feet, and seemed to become inflated eight to twelve times its original size. His ears grew long enough to touch the ground, and acted as a prop in holding him up. His hair was long, shaggy, and snow white. Meantime, he beckoned to Slim to come near and help him. Slim was praying and begging for mercy all the while, and confessing to all the petty thievery he had ever committed. He even promised never to steal chickens, or melons in that part of the country again, but the ghost still beckoned to him.

Finally, the specter emitted a macabre sigh, grew very tall, and became as narrow as a stake rope. Its body stretched and broke into pieces. The pieces hung in the air for a moment and then disappeared.

Some of the older settlers in the neighborhood said there was once a tradition in this community about an old Dutchman who was robbed and murdered under the very tree where Slim had fallen asleep, but there were no Dutch people living in the neighborhood at this time to confirm the story.

Good Cow Bess

ONCE A WEEK, a relay of ranchmen and their wives gathered at the Bruce Ranch to help milk old Bess, the prize Jersey cow of the community. This was a tremendous job for all concerned. Under the shade of a giant oak tree, three to five tons of cotton seed mixed with meal were placed

in a big trough before her. Back of this was a big vat four feet wide, over which old Bess stood astride while being milked. The vat led down a hill, a quarter of a mile long, carrying the milk into an enormous tank.

When Good Cow Bess started to eat her feed, four of the farmers began milking her. After the milk began flowing, they stepped aside because it was a known fact that afterward, the milk would just keep running out in four large streams into the vat. It was so rich that another relay of farmers stood along the sides of the vat with shovels, scooping out the butter collected there. They had to work fast or the butter would clog up the vat in places, causing the milk to overflow.

The women stood at nearby tables molding and wrapping the butter. Bunk Huggins and his father, Herb, and two other men carried the butter in wheelbarrows to these tables. They were kept very busy for no less than twenty-four hours each time Good Cow Bess was milked.

The only thing that worried everyone, especially the cow, was the heel flies, as big as pigeons, flying around and stinging her. She swished her tail often, but one swish knocked a man down. So, to keep anyone from being hurt, the men took cables and tied her tail to the trunk of the giant oak. However, four or five men stood by the tree with sharp axes ready to cut the cables in case she started to walk up a few paces, as they did not want Good Cow Bess to uproot this tree.

At one time, some of the men had brought their guns along to shoot these pesky heel flies; but the women persuaded them that it was a dangerous thing to have the weapons about, since there were so many children playing around the place.

Bunk Huggins declared he would knock a couple of "the durn heel flies down with his baseball bat if he did not have to wheel butter." However, no one ever paid much attention to Bunk; he was just a harmless little man of the neighborhood. He was no less than thirty years old, but had the mind of a child of six.

Some people said he was born a half-wit; others said his mother had dropped him from his baby buggy when he was three months old. Neither story was ever confirmed. However, Old Man Lunkins, who was still angry with Bunk for knocking over one of his bee hives, said that Bunk just lacked six weeks of being born an idiot.

When someone inquired why he did it, Bunk said in his lazy drawl, "Wal, I jes' tuck my baseball bat an' knocked it offen the block to see whut the durn things wuz doin' goin' in an' outen that box all day long."

Years before that, some neighbor had given him a baseball bat for Christmas; from that time on, Bunk carried it with him everywhere he went.

Bunk was an excellent cow hand when his father was with him, but some of the people were afraid of the baseball bat.

Now, the milk from old Bess was carried to town in trucks built with giant tanks on them similar to gas and oil trucks. It was thought for awhile by some of the leading citizens in the community that the government would improve the situation by building a pipeline from the Bruce Ranch to the railroad station to carry nothing but milk. This, however, was never done. But the railroad officials did help by sending a special train through there once a week to carry nothing but milk and butter to the northern markets.

Jingling Spurs

STRAIGHT THROUGH the pasture lands, no more than four miles away from the Bruce Ranch, was the old Slincke place. This farm had an enormous, two-story house — once painted white — many outhouses, and about a hundred acres of excellent farming land. The owners had no heirs in America and had gone back to Germany on a visit. They stayed so long that the yard grew up in tall weeds. Moreover, small bushes and shrubs of all kinds were spread over the fields now. The colored folks who lived near this old home declared that they had seen "hants" about the place.

People of the community were beginning to wonder what had happened to the old German couple, now absent for more than ten years.

Early one morning just before good daylight, Jerd Simpson rode up to the Bruce Ranch. He seemed to have something serious on his mind. He immediately asked Uncle Billie if he had noticed his sheep in the last two days. Uncle Billie replied that he always looked over his ranch every day.

"Well, you shore better come and take a squint at about fifty head of yore sheep now," Jerd said. "I just looked at 'em and blinked my eyes to make shore of what I seen. They are in the same fix as I found mine," he concluded.

Uncle Billie hurried to the sheep sheds, thinking that he would find fifty or more of his sheep stretched out dead of blackleg, or hoof and mouth disease, or some other malady common to livestock. He was amazed and astounded to find that the sheep had been completely sheared. Moreover, the shearing was different to any he had ever seen. Their coats were as sleek as the bare skin. In fact, there was no wool left on them.

"Well, they are as clean as a washboard after a long wash day," commented Uncle Billie.

At this moment, five to ten other ranchmen and cowboys arrived on the scene; Bunk Huggins, panting and all out of breath, brought up the rear on a stick horse.

"Are you-uns gonna hang sombudy? Can't I ride along?" he said.

But no one paid much attention to him. The ranchmen were angry enough to hang to an old hickory tree on Frog Gully the first wool-stealing suspect they found. A limb on this gnarled old tree had had one rope on it before, in very early times. But no one ever discussed this, and no one seemed to know much about it.

"Who in the world would be shearing sheep now? However, it is near time for shearing," said one cowboy.

"Whoever did that shearing had more gall then hot dogs have holidays," said Ab Jones, Jr.

One farmer said he had traced the thieves toward the Slincke farm; he had seen very strange tracks leading in that direction.

"You know that would be a good hiding place for any thief, as it is in somewhat of a desolate place," agreed another. "And he could bag the wool there, hide it away, and carry it off some night in large trucks," he concluded.

The men jumped on their ponies, let down fences, and started over to the Slincke farm. They had not gone far when they picked up a trail leading from the Bruce Ranch. Even a few wisps of wool were found hanging to the bushes along the way. This evidence fired everyone with enthusiasm, as they were certain now they would catch these mysterious thieves who had been going about from ranch to ranch shearing sheep each night now for a week or more.

As they came near the old place, the country seemed to become lonely and quiet.

"Now, men," said Jerd Simpson, taking over the leadership, "we will leave our horses here in this post oak mott, and walk quietly up to the house. Before we go, however, we must tie broom weeds over each of our spurs so they will not jingle. We must have everything very quiet as we sneak in."

The ranchmen and farmers soon surrounded the outhouses by hiding behind some scrubby bushes. They waited for fifteen minutes or more, thinking they might see someone about the place, hear someone talking.

Bunk Huggins had ridden over on the same horse with Old Man Simpson.

"Jes' give me a chanc't," he said, "I allow I can go in thet 'ar' ole shed, an' knock all the durn thieves crazier 'an a bedbug in karsen oil with this 'er baseball bat," he replied to the private conversations around him.

The men had to restrain him. They blamed Old Man Simpson for letting Bunk come, but the old man said that he "allus felt sorra fer the lad 'cause he was one of nature's bad blunders."

After about fifteen minutes of listening and hearing nothing, the men decided to give the signal to go in the place together from all sides. Presently, though, they heard peculiar noises coming from the house. It sounded as if someone were stripping the gears to his car. Also, the front door was opened about an inch, but no one was visible.

"Now is our time to fall on them and capture them by surprise," whispered one of the men.

Some of the ranchmen hurried quietly to the back, while some of the others went to the front. They tried to open the door cautiously, but it made a creaking noise. Just at this moment, two great moths lunged forward and knocked the men down! Two other ranchmen came up to help their friends, but were slugged by other moths! Then it seemed that hundreds of them came out of the house, almost trampling the intruders to death. The wall adjoining the front door was knocked down! Small ones, large ones, old ones, young ones, crippled ones, and all kinds flooded the porch and yard. The ranchmen had to flee for their lives in this melee!

The size and number of the moths would have astounded the Pied Piper, if he had been present. These enormous moths had eaten the rugs off the floors, the paper from the walls, all the clothes in the house; in fact, everything made of paper or rags. Then they had become so ravenously hungry for wool that they had started shearing the sheep on all the surrounding ranches with their sharp teeth.

Some of the moths had just got back from their nightly shearings, and were cleaning their feet and preening their wings when the ranchmen arrived. Hence, the noise like gears being stripped.

There were a few wisps of wool in a back room left there by the younger moths. They had not been able to eat quite all the wool which their parents had brought them.

The Ranch Garden

THIS PARTICULAR SPRING, Aunt Sue planted her garden in a small field beyond the railroad tracks. She said it would be safer there from the chickens. She planted Irish potatoes, spinach, popcorn, cabbage, snap beans, peas, lettuce and other

vegetables that gardeners plant in that section of the country in the spring.

One day when the garden was in full production, Hank Jenkins, a neighbor, discovered a big ditch on his land. It ran back into Aunt Sue's garden. Now, he was very curious to know the cause of this gully. Even the sheep had been walking up this ditch, going under the fence into the garden, and feasting on fine vegetables. Hank came to the house to get someone to go with him to the garden.

He and Uncle Jake hurried down there, only to find that a sweet potato had grown so large it had cracked the ground open, making an excavation no less than six feet wide and ten feet deep! It was astounding! The big crack ran over into Hank's land, causing a creek to form. Furthermore, Hank had come to the ranch to make another complaint. It was that this same " 'tater vine in Miz Bruce's garden had run a mile over into his paster; that one of his best milk cows had gotten tangled up in it and might nigh died."

He said that he "allowed that 'tater vines did not make good milk no way, so could he cut 'em up?" He needed some "fence postes fer the longest, an' would be willin' to chop the vines the right lengths fer haff uv 'em if Miz Bruce didn't care." Hank got several good loads of posts from the vines, not to mention the firewood, too.

Now, the watermelon vines seemed to be racing also that spring. They ran so fast the little melons, not being able to keep up, had to sit down to rest. While they were resting, their stems grew to be about twenty feet long. Then the melons began to grow. They grew so large that a cottontail rabbit hollowed out one of the seeds, and made a home in it for her and her five little bunnies.

Of course, these melons took the blue ribbon at the County Fair; and people from other states came to view, with wonder, these great melons. A professor from some Northern university, visiting the Fair, said these melons, he was sure, belonged to the age of mastodons. Some people, never hearing about mastodons, thought he meant that a new plant had been developed.

Also, that spring, some other vegetables did rather well, too. One week the rain washed the spinach so slick and clean that when the sun shone out, it reflected its color on the low hanging clouds and there were green clouds floating over the sky for two hours or more.

But Ab Jones, Sr., accompanied by Ab, Jr., had a complaint to make about the spinach leaves hanging over the garden fence. He said one particular leaf had become so large that it was shading more than ten acres of his young cotton, and "everybudy knowed thet shade weren't no good fer cotton. It ort to be cut down." Anyways, he "seen a boll weevil leading her whole family of thirteen young 'uns back under that same bunch of spinach to stay until late summer."

"They were as big as a house cat," said Ab, Jr. "Why, really, they looked like a string of miniature elephants moving across that cotton field. I saw the old one bore a hole in the ground, and the young 'uns ran inside; then she backed in, and was ready to fight anything coming her way. About that time," continued Ab, Jr., "I saw a coon come up, and when he spied the boll weevil, right then there was a fight. The coon used all of his ingenuity to get the boll weevil to come out and fight honestly; but the boll weevil only reached out her bill. She nicked the coon's ear, jerked off some fur, cut the coon's nose, trimmed his claws, and left a lump on the coon's head," concluded Ab, Jr.

Now, this coon was Aunt Emma's pet. He was so subdued and humbled from the fight that he sneaked into the house like a beaten prize fighter. He stayed hidden under the bed for two whole days. He would come out only at nights when the family was in bed. Aunt Emma and Uncle Jake used "Coonie," as they called him, for a watchdog.

"Caze dat coon sho' let us know when somebody come 'roun,'" said Aunt Emma. "He run all ober dis house a-growlin' an' jumpin' an' lookin' 'roun,' 'til we see what's de mattah," she explained.

It took two whole days to saw the spinach leaf down, and by the end of the following week, it was cut and stacked like great sheets of metal.

Uncle Jake hurried to the house one morning and seemed to be very excited. He had been to the garden. Not being able to see well, Uncle Jake thought at first that one of these streamlined passenger trains had been derailed, and had hurled a coach over the fence into the garden. The coach was still moving, too, he thought. But coming closer, he saw that it was only an enormous tomato worm! What made Uncle Jake so angry about the whole thing was that the worm was rolling some of the garden's finest English peas in front of him toward his den. Uncle Jake had cultivated those peas, especially, and he had found one of them to weigh fifty pounds, not counting the others in the same pod.

He hurried back to the garden with his shotgun loaded and ready to dispose of the worm. He found that the worm was traveling at the rate of seventy-five feet a loop — as worms travel. Moreover, the worm was too far away to shoot. He was probably at a distance of fifty loops or more. Uncle Jake, who was suffering from "de rheumatiz," could not follow it. The last he saw of the worm was a great loop in the distance, as it went over a hill. It was still rolling the peas in front of it, too.

Aunt Sue had insisted on planting some curly mustard that spring, and it grew rather luxuriantly. A part of one plant had leaves that grew over the garden fence into the goat pasture. A herd of goats, seeing the opportunity, started running up and down playing on them. They were able, in this way, to run over the fence into the garden. The kids in the herd liked to play hide-and-go-seek among the curls in the leaves. However, some of the goats with more destructive intentions began to nibble on the edges of the leaves. It was a week before Aunt Sue noticed that the goats had not only eaten up most of the mustard, but all the wire netting which enclosed that side of the garden fence.

One hot afternoon in midsummer when the garden was beginning to dry up, Aunt Sue walked out into the back yard. A loud noise like the crack of a rifle sounded. She listened for a moment, and decided it was some of the ranch children out shooting rabbits.

But, crack! There it went again! It sounded as if it came from the garden. She hurried off in that direction, wondering as she went along if some of the renters had had a misunderstanding among themselves and had decided to just shoot it out. It never had happened before on the Bruce Ranch.

As she hurried along, the shooting grew worse and worse. She thought once that she should run back to the house and call for help. However, she hoped some of the other ranch people would hear the noise and come, too. Could she afford to go on, and maybe get shot with a stray bullet? Nevertheless, she was a brave woman who feared nothing; so she ran on. As she came nearer and nearer, she heard some pitiful cries, too. She looked up and saw some cloud-like flecks flying through the air. The noise of shooting almost drowned out the pitiful cries.

"Someone is certainly in trouble," she said as she ran faster.

When she came near the fence, she saw a sight she had never dreamed of! Her popcorn was popping ferociously and flying through the air in all directions! After it had popped,

each grain was large enough to fit comfortably into a me-
dium size dish pan. Great drifts of it began to settle like
snow against the garden fence. It lay out in the pasture in
great piles.

Bunk Huggins was there having the best time of his life
— he thought. Of course, he had his baseball bat with him,
as usual. When the fluffy grains shot over his way — and
they certainly did come thick and fast — he knocked them
as he would have a baseball. This popping continued for
the next hour. Aunt Sue could do nothing about it so she
stood for awhile, and watched in awe. The big fluffy grains,
some yellow but most of them white, sailed through the air
and landed gracefully as if they were parachutes.

"The sun was just too hot," she said. "And now all of
my fine seed are gone."

She forgot about the pitiful cries during the thickest of
the popping, but suddenly she heard them again, and they
sounded more distressing and louder than ever. She hurried
through the garden over to the other side near the fence,
where she found five goats bogged down in a big, overripe
red tomato! It was laughable, yet serious for the goats. One
was a kid standing on an island made by one tomato seed
in the middle of the slush. All the goats were crying
piteously. They had climbed over the fence on some of the
old curly mustard leaves still hanging there, now a greenish
brown color and almost dry. Aunt Sue went quickly to the
house, followed by Bunk. They must get some help, and dig
the goats out of the tomato.

As they were walking along, Bunk said, "I heerd them
goats a-cryin' an' started to the house to tell ye about it. I
allowed you-uns wanted to know. But wen I seed the corn
a-bustin' an' a flyin' in a air, I got fun hittin' the durn stuff
with my baseball bat, an' clean forgot 'bout them goats, the

frazzlin' things. I had lotsa fun, too. Durn goats always into sumpin."

All the neighbors were invited over that evening to a popcorn party.

Furthermore, Aunt Sue decided to shade her popcorn the next season until it was gathered.

Branding Dogies

EVERY SPRING, the cattle that had
no brands were rounded up
from the four corners of the
Bruce Ranch. The familiar seven-
o (7o) Bruce brand was
placed on the right
hip of each dogie.

The cattle were put in
large corrals until they were
branded. The old method
of lassoing cattle, tying
them down,

and placing a red hot branding iron on them, had long ago been outmoded at the Bruce Ranch by a new, streamlined method.

A cowboy sat in a small cultivator seat hooked over the sides of a tall narrow passage leading from one corral to another. This passage resembled the entrance to a dipping vat. In fact, the first one built was the old dipping vat remodeled. The cowboy wore boots fitting snugly around his ankles. The heels of these custom made boots were of iron, and the brand seven-o (7o) bradded to each of them. A gas torch was securely attached to both sides of the narrow passage where the cowboy heated his brands. Of course, the torches were placed too high to frighten or molest the cattle.

The cowboy sat with each heel over a torch for a few moments, until the brands became red hot. Then the work started. The cattle, one head at a time, were driven through the narrow passage, or chute. The cowboy branded one cow with one heel of his boot, and the next cow with the other heel in lightning precision.

The dogies came through so fast that the friction of the branding iron on their coats of hair caused the branding irons to stay red hot. Old Saint Vitus, had he been present, would have been ashamed of his own slothful movements in comparison.

One man could brand five thousand cattle per day. This new method of branding cattle was produced, or as the modern thinkers might say, was the "brainchild" of old man Ab Jones.

He had sent his oldest son, Ab, Jr., off to A.&M. College to learn more about farming, hog, cattle, and sheep raising. Then, one holiday near the end of the last term of Ab's college career when the old man went to visit him, he found Ab, Jr. doing a tap dance that he had learned from some of the college boys. Surrounded by a group of admirers,

Ab, Jr. was fracturing the floorboards at the moment when his father walked in on the scene.

Old man Jones was so angry he took Ab away from college that very day, in spite of the persuasions of both the faculty and the Board of Education. When the old man was asked to explain his decision concerning his son, he spat and said:

"I allow I sent my son to college to train his head, his hands, and not his feet with them new fangled-foot-scraping-works of the devil, and besides, I don't want him a larnin' that furrin' stuff call Latin."

Ab, Jr. had been displaying his Latin abilities before his little brothers, Bud and Asa, and it had angered the old man to hear anything but English spoken around his house.

The old man then changed his wad of tobacco from one side of his mouth to the other and continued, "What would a hawg know about *amo* or a somethin' whatever it is, if Ab called a hawg? Didn't we have enough troubles already with them furriners? Didn't Thomas A. Edison say when he was President of these United States fer us to stay clean outen furrin 'tanglements, as it were unconstitutional? I got a big book whut tells all about it."

"Pa, Thomas A. Edison wuz not President of the United States, he were the President of Detroit er Michigan er some uv the other northern countries," said meek Mrs. Jones, trying to be helpful.

"Yes, he were, too. It says so in that leakopedia I got fum that book agent. You knowed I let him spend the night at our house jes' to git that book," he argued.

Nevertheless, Old Man Jones had made good use of Ab, Jr.'s learning the tap dance, and was secretly pleased with himself when he thought out this new method of branding cattle. He called it tap branding, since the method was learned from tap dancing.

Around the Campfire

EACH YEAR on his birthday, Uncle Billie 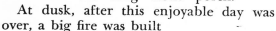 gave a barbecue for his friends, especially, those who had driven up The Trail. Eight to twelve of those old friends, with their families, came from distant ranches to spend the night. There was plenty of room, as beds for the men folks were made on the long front porch.

At dusk, after this enjoyable day was over, a big fire was built

again in the barbecue pit; a washpot of coffee was put on to brew; and these old cowboys with their children and grandchildren gathered around to hear some of the Old Trail Drivers retell their experiences of going up The Trail. Uncle Billie always led in these narrations, telling his favorite story first. Most people knew what it would be, but they were always thrilled at his manner of relating it.

"I had four or five cowboys to help me with one of the largest herds of longhorn cattle that I ever drove up the Old Chisholm Trail. Besides these hands, I had the cook and the water boy, both colored, and my two brothers, Charles and Robert Bruce. I always dreaded to go through any Indian Territory because sometimes the Indians were bad about going into my chuck wagon, and taking my provisions; and sometimes they were hard to deal with, too.

"Occasionally, we would travel nearly all night to get through Indian Territory quickly. Early one morning, we were sleeping peacefully after a long hard drive part of the night before, when I was awakened to see an old squaw trying to open the provision box on my chuck wagon. My saddle horse, hobbled near my bed, had snorted until he had awakened me. He did not like the smell of the Indians.

"Now, I had prepared specially for this moment. I had gotten some Mexican jumping beans out of Mexico. They were as large as a small ostrich egg. I had them placed in a grass sack in the provision compartment of the chuck wagon. When this old squaw climbed on the wagon, the jarring shook the beans and started them to jumping. This old thief opened the sack, thinking she would find small pigs or chickens in it. When the first bean jumped out of the sack, she stared in amazement. She knew what beans were, but the size and jumps were beyond her experience. When the next two jumped, she screamed with horror; almost fell from the wagon and ran whooping through the woods, jabbering something between her whoops."

"All the rest of the day, The Trail was devoid of Indians. We knew they were about, however, for the little colored water boy, rolling his eyes back and forth, declared that he saw painted feathers sticking up through the bushes all day.

"On this same trip one evening as I was traveling along up The Trail," he continued, "a very black cloud spread over the sky. I knew we were in for trouble of some sort, maybe hail. I hastily sent word to all the cowboys to round up the cattle and stand by and try to keep them from scattering in all directions. When a big hailstorm came up, it sometimes took us a week to find all the cattle. Moreover, a cowboy does well to protect himself from the falling stones. I have unsaddled my horse many a time and have gotten under the saddle for protection. However, this particular afternoon, there was only a great downpour. The rain was so thick — and it was getting dark besides — that I could scarcely see fifty feet ahead of me.

"The cattle were hard to hold in one place, so we drove them slowly along. We finally came to a tall embankment. It looked as if it might be a mound built for the railroad. However, we could see daylight under it in one place. I decided that this opening was made for a bridge or an underpass. I did not think we had come to a tunnel in a mountain. If there was such a place, I had no recollection of it on my previous trips, and I did not think we were that far off The Trail in spite of the rainstorm. However, I did not know.

"The opening was several hundred feet long, and fifty to seventy-five feet high. It was raining so terribly hard by this time that we could tell absolutely nothing about this passage. We drove our cattle through it. All the while, the cattle were snorting, running, and horning each other. We wanted to stay under this tunnel or opening; but since the cattle hurried through, we could not linger. Furthermore, we did not know when the water might begin to rise in this supposedly low place. When we were safely through it, one of the cowboys who brought up the rear came rushing up to tell us that the mound had moved. The opening then was larger than ever.

"By this time, the rain had subsided somewhat and we could see farther ahead. We thought maybe a flood had come and moved this tall embankment, but looking more closely, we were amazed to see it moving slowly over the territory. It was an enormous lobo wolf! He was our mound and was carrying five or six head of cattle off in his mouth. However, the cattle had passed under him safely to the other side; he had crouched there during the downpour, but the men had made so much noise driving the cattle that it had aroused him.

" 'Old Lobo,' as he was called by some people, had been hunted by the government agents for years. Some people would report his being in their vicinity, but when the government men arrived with their cannon he would be in some other state. He had thrived on cattle, sheep, and goats for years, running over the ranges. This great wolf had been shot many times, but an ordinary gun did him no harm; the government must shoot him with a cannon. As he was very wild, he never came near where there were any homes; he never molested people."

When Uncle Billie had finished this story, the women started serving coffee. They passed the cups out to all the men but Uncle Billie. They asked him what he would take. He just laughed and said he would take a Dolly Varden.

"What is that?" asked one of the ladies.

"That is one of my specials," he said with a broad grin

on his face. "A glass of water with a big bubble in it."

"Ho! Ho!" cried Bunk Huggins, who was sitting near with both ears and mouth wide open. "I think it wuz some buttermilk an' pepper sauce kinda mixed with guinea giz- zards. You tole me oncet it 'ud make my whiskers grow, an' I been havin' a durn time a-findin' them gizzards ever sincet," he said.

After the coffee was served and everyone seemed wide awake and feeling gay again, Uncle Tollie Lemons was asked to tell some of his favorite experiences.

Uncle Tollie was tall and slender. He always wore a black Stetson, a white shirt, a dark vest, and dark trousers. When he talked, his goatee wriggled in a ludicrous manner and his muttonchop whiskers jumped up and down. He chewed tobacco constantly, and often changed the quid from one side of his mouth to the other, especially, while he was talking. His given name was Tolliver. The children loved to hear him tell about his experiences, and they liked the rolls of stick candy that he brought them. Watching his goatee move when he talked amused them greatly.

"Well," he said. "I started driving cattle when I was only eleven years old. When I was thirteen, I could rope any yearling on the range. At eighteen, I was a champion at roping and tying steers. I started driving cattle up The Trail for a neighborhood when I was nineteen. When I was twenty- five, I drove up The Trail with my own outfit. We made The Trail more than twenty times. There were many saloons and gambling dives in the few towns where we traveled up The Trail. A cowboy was always glad to get to some town to buy a new suit of clothes though, and see something else besides cattle and other cowboys. I have seen some Trail Drivers, who had worn out the seat of their trousers from constant riding, sneak off their ponies and walk backwards into the first dry goods store they found, and buy a new suit of clothes.

"I always paid off my boys before we came to town so they could buy what they wanted and needed. In one town which we will call Squedunk, a famous gambler owned and operated all the saloons and gambling dives. He was both hated and feared by most people. He was a law unto himself. He had a keen eye, was quick on the draw, and could shoot out a squirrel's eye at six hundred yards. This gambler had his henchmen stationed all over town. They kept him well informed as to which Trail Driver would be in, and at what time he would arrive. I never believed in gambling nor going around such places, but I always felt it was my duty to look after the cowboys in my outfit. I hated to see them skinned in a gambling game. Some of them had families who needed their money.

"This slick gambler was called Ozzie Spranglon. He seemed to be everywhere at once. He was so hard on the men who worked for him that they feared him as much as death.

"One evening while we were in Squedunk, I was going from one dive to another trying to round up my cow hands. I saw Ozzie coming toward me. 'Goodness, he is a hard-looking, bloody cuss,' I said to myself. As he came near, someone at the bar over on the right shot at him. When the shot struck Ozzie's shadow, it glanced back and hit the bar counter! He spoke to me politely, passed on, and pretended not to have noticed the shooting!

"The next morning, we hit The Trail earlier than usual. When we had traveled for about half a day, one of the boys turned back to tell me that there was another outfit about a day ahead of us; that he had seen three covered wagons going over one of the hills in the distance. I hurried to the front and went on ahead. I spent the night in a lonely place and was awakened to find black ants as large as house cats walking over me, trying to drag my saddle out from under my head. The next day at noon, I caught up with the outfit the cowboy had told me about, only to find three dry land terrapins as large as covered wagons traveling slowly up The Old Chisholm Trail."

To the Rescue

ONE DAY Mrs. Simpson walked out
to the woodpile to get some
kindling and wood. She was going to build a fire to cook the
midday meal. Mr. Simpson usually
came in from the field about
twelve-thirty for lunch.
He was always hot, tired, and hungry. He was busy that day digging his Irish potatoes.

  Mrs. Simpson had
filled her cook apron with

WALTER
McKINNEY

kindling and was beginning to pick up the wood when she heard a noise behind her. She turned about quickly to see Mr. Lund's old billy goat standing on his hind legs with a piece of red paper in his mouth, muttering. Now, this old goat meant to fight Mrs. Simpson. She was terrified. Wondering how to get past him back into the yard, she quickly threw down her wood and kindling. Because of a rheumatic pain in her back, she could run very poorly.

The old goat was backing now with his head down and his neck bowed, getting ready to make a run at her. Mrs. Simpson jerked off her cook apron, and threw it over the old billy goat's head. While he was busy with the cook apron, she hurried into the yard and latched the gate securely.

Her snuffbox with all the snuff she had was in her apron pocket! The goat tore up the apron immediately, and chewed up a part of it. Then bleating loudly and daring her to come outside the fence, he came and lay down against the gate. Mrs. Simpson wanted that snuffbox more than anything she had wanted for a very long time. She had taken enough time to enjoy only one dip of snuff that morning. She had intended to sit down to rest, and take a dip while the stove was getting hot. She was alone. Trudy, her daughter, had gone off in the buggy to the little store four miles away; and it would be several hours before she would return.

Mrs. Simpson thought of many plans to get her snuffbox, but none of them worked. However, she was happy to know that the goat, as yet, had not discovered it. She had almost given up the idea of getting her precious snuffbox, when Bunk Huggins appeared on the scene with his baseball bat! She was glad to see him, for once. Bunk had yellow dust on him from head to foot.

"Where you-uns been all this time, Bunk?" she asked.

"I wuz over in a paster when I seed two bumblebees a fightin'! They flew up in a air when they seen I wuz gonna hit 'em with my bat, but one uv 'em drapped a load of thet yaller meal they pack on their laigs ret on top o' my haid. It musta been twenty-five pound or mo! I couldn't see how to hit the durn things, an' they flew clean away."

"I shore wish you'd fetch my snuffbox fum out thar in thet woodpile an' make thet ole goat uv Mr. Lund's go 'way," said Mrs. Simpson.

Bunk not only made the goat leave, but brought her snuffbox and a big load of wood into the house for her. He made yellow tracks all through the house. He walked through the kitchen, and the dining room and on into the parlor. Trudy found him there looking at the family album when she came back from the community store. She was very angry for two reasons: First, because the floors had been tracked up with pollen; and second, because Bunk had commented to her on a young man's picture in the album.

"Who is thet ar' feller a standin' behin' thet whitewashed fence?" he asked, dropping pollen all over the picture.

"You knowed my pappy wore a collar like 'at," he continued, looking seriously at Trudy. "He dressed in his Sunday pants with his big white collar on, an' went a-courtin' the Widder Bowers las' night, but she tuck a broom an' clean runned him outen 'er house; an' 'er kids sicked old Zero, her yaller houn', on to him. Pappy said that he'd aimed to marry with her cause she's got a home an' after they wuz married, he'd burn some o' the durn outhouses down to git the surance so's he'd hev' money then. He said he'd buy me a new suit o 'close, an' a big white collar, too, an' give me a whole dollar," he continued. "Who'd you say this 'er feller wuz?

"Lookit his mouf! I bet wen he kisses a gal, his mouf

sounds lik' a cow a pullin' her foot outen a bog hole!"

Trudy wanted to laugh about Bunk's father's courtship with the Widow Bowers, but she was too angry. That was her boy friend's picture. He wore a tall white collar and a small bow which was very stylish. She did not want anyone making derogatory remarks about her boy friend.

About that time, Mr. Simpson came to the house in a big rush to get the block and tackle. Some of his Irish potatoes were so large he could not lift them. One in particular weighed more then two hundred pounds. Bunk took his bat and went along with Mr. Simpson to the field, and left Trudy smouldering in anger over her dirty house and boy friend's picture.

A Short Cut Home

AUNT SAMANTHA, who was colored
and who weighed no less than
four hundred pounds, de-
cided she would like to ride home
from church in the buggy with
Aunt Emma. Uncle Jake
and Aunt Emma were kind,
Christian, old colored people
who passed right by her house
every Sunday going
to church. She and Aunt
Emma always had plenty to talk
about. The colored

people's church was not so far from Aunt Samantha's home. Aunt Samantha did not take this riding notion very often, but when she did, then Uncle Jake had to walk home, taking the nearest cut through by the old pond.

Uncle Jake happened to have on his new shoes that day, and it was the first time he had worn them out in public.

He had said to his wife, "I'm gonna wear dem new shoes terday so's all dem niggahs can see 'em; an' I hopes dey squeak louder dan dey did de fust time I done wore 'em roun' dis house now."

Aunt Emma replied, "Jake, dem shoes sho' do squeak. Yo' bettah put some goose greas' on 'em so's dey will be quiet. You all will rouse de whole neighborhood wid 'dem. All de folks will think Mr. Lund's ole wagon done come 'long de road, a-squak, a-squak, a-squawkin!"

"No, I wants de whole country ter know I'se got a pair o' new shoes, and 'sides dat's bad luck ter grease de squawks outen shoes.

"And, Emme, you all know sumpin? I'se gwine ter walk ret down to de front pew to sit so's all 'de folks will see dem shoes," he continued.

"Jake Smith, de debbil done got in yo' blood, clean to yo' toes," she answered.

"Emme, put dat seegar de boss done gimme in my coat pocket so's I'll look mo' constu'tonal. All de men whut wu'k in de city has dem in dey coat pockets."

Uncle Jake never smoked cigars except on Sundays, and not then unless someone had given him one. The owner of the ranch had given Jake a fine cigar the day before. Uncle Jake was a favorite hand on this ranch. He smoked a cob pipe incessantly.

At church, he made his word good. It was a trifle late when he and Aunt Emma arrived at church, but he walked down the aisle to a front seat. His shoes made so much noise that most everyone turned in their seats as he passed. Even Deacon Brown, who sat on the rostrum, was aroused for the moment from his peaceful slumbers. Moreover, the parson waited for Uncle Jake to be seated.

There were loud whispers of admiration all along the aisle as Uncle Jake walked past. This pleased him very much.

When church was over, Uncle Jake found that he had to walk home. However, being the cynosure of all wistful eyes, he strutted about in his new shoes among the congregation, talking to the different brothers and sisters. During this time, he managed to place one foot prominently on a chair or bench inside the church, or a stump on the outside, to show off his new shoes.

Aunt Emma called him several times, asking him to start for home, but seeing it was useless, she finally said that she, Samantha, and little Moses, her nephew who lived with them, would ride on.

However, it looked for a time as if Samantha would not be able to get into the buggy. After several trials, she at last pulled herself in. Then Aunt Emma climbed into what space there was left on the other side of the buggy seat. Little Moses stood up in the back to ride, and with a cluck to the fat, gotch-eared, little roan-colored pony, the buggy started to move slowly down the road with one side showing extreme weightiness.

Meantime, Uncle Jake happened to remember they were having boiled backbone and hominy, the first fresh hog meat of the season, for dinner, so he thought he had better start for home. Samantha, on her own volition — and she had a great knack for such things — might decide to go on home with Aunt Emma for dinner. Then Uncle Jake might not get his share of the eats.

He set off through the woods, and was soon near the old pond. No one ever paid much attention to this pond. It was thirty or forty feet deep in some places, the water mostly stagnant. Cattle, when not grazing, stood around the pond most of the time, fighting heel flies. After big rains, once in awhile, some of the neighborhood children fished there for perch.

Now, there were a few wild tales about this old pond. It was said that one year when the dust storms came down from the great northern dust bowls, the atmosphere was so dark around this pool that the little frogs could not see how to catch flies and other insects. Consequently, they nearly starved to death. Finally, though, as a last resort, several of them left the pond and went to the woods in search of food. They found many lightning bugs, filled their pouches full of them, and returned to the pond. The lightning bugs illuminated the frogs' bodies, and sent out such a glow around them that the other little frogs were able to catch flies, dirt-daubers, etc., and were thus saved from starvation. Even the larger frogs hunting flies, by this artificial light, were able to exist until the dust storms subsided.

Another old tale that passed from generation to generation among the natives was that the dust got into the eyes of the mosquitoes that inhabited the pond, and blinded some of them so badly that they wandered into deep mud, bogged down, and died of suffocation. Other mosquitoes, having dust in their eyes, just sat where they were so long that they took arthritis in their knees and could not walk for weeks. Others were afflicted with pinkeye, carried by the dust.

Jerd Simpson's grandfather had confirmed the veracity of this last statement, and Grandpap Simpson was a favorite man of the neighborhood. However, everyone in the community knew that pinkeye was a malady known only among schoolchildren.

Just as Uncle Jake came to the pond, his feet started hurting him. He grunted loudly and sat down.

"Yo' sho' gonna haf' ter com' off, yo' squawkers. I cain' stan' yo' no mo' now! Dat bunion feel lak' it gwine ter bus', an' dem corns, dey sho' tellin' dese shoes when ter com' off," he said to himself. Then he quickly pulled off his shoes and socks, tied his shoes together, stuffed his socks into his pockets, and looked all about him.

He continued, "I sho hopes Mr. Lund's ole billy goat doan' see me. I lef' my walkin' stick hom' dis time and dat ole goat sho' go whar he please and hit whar he please, too!"

With these words, he slung his shoes over one shoulder, stood up, and continued his journey home barefoot.

Soon the heel flies, that had been a scourge to cattle for years in this immediate vicinity, discovered Uncle Jake's bare heels, and were swarming around him. He knocked at them several times, but to no avail. They alighted on his heels as he walked along.

Subsequently, two big bullfrogs, weighing no less than one hundred and fifty pounds each, saw their chance for a quick dinner. After Uncle Jake was several hundred yards or more past the pond, they jumped out and started hopping along following him. Now, it was a known fact in the community that when these bullfrogs croaked, the people thought it was thunder, and would rush out to see where the rain cloud "was making."

Each bullfrog, staying at a safe distance of twenty-five yards or more from Uncle Jake, started lapping the heel flies from his heels. They followed along behind him for a mile or more, lapping away. In fact, the frogs lapped so many that Uncle Jake's heels became badly chapped from the moisture of their tongues. When he arrived home, the blood was oozing out of each heel.

A Straying Dogie

IT WAS UNUSUALLY late in the spring that year when the cowboys on the Bruce Ranch began to round up the dogies for their yearly branding.

Everything in the Big White House was in a stir and a shuffle. "Big White House" was the name given to the ranch owner's home. It was the center of all the ranch activities, just a quarter of a mile from the barns, the sheds, and the corrals.

Everything seemed sleepy that spring; even the field larks were late about coming to dig up the corn in the roasting ear patch belonging to the Big White House. There were a few larks around the fields, but the little stalks of corn had just about outgrown them. Some larks were hunting out the roots of the tardy little stalks, digging up the old sprouted grains.

One particular spring morning, an enormous lark flew into the middle of the corn patch. His bill was no less than a foot long, but it was not incongruously large considering the proportions of the rest of his body. He seemed to know exactly where grains of corn and worms wore located. He knifed his huge beak into the ground, and drew up an earthworm as large as a big cable. He started pulling on this earthworm and backing. He followed this same procedure with each pull until he reached the pasture fence. Then he flew up on the barbed wire and continued pulling on the worm until he was able to drag it over the fence into the pasture. Still, a major portion of the earthworm remained in the ground. Nevertheless, the huge lark had pulled out no less than one hundred and fifty feet of the worm, and was still busily engaged when a straying dogie happened to rush over that way. The dogie was not only running away from the herd, and the cowboys who were rounding up cattle, but he was trying to evade a persistent heel fly. Of course, most of the heel flies in that immediate vicinity were as large as pigeons. None of the natives paid much attention to them, but most newcomers, when they saw one flying around, supposed that someone in the community had a flock of pigeons.

The dogie, running at top speed, got his feet tangled up in some of the loops and curves of the earthworm, and ran stumbling behind a great oak tree just in time to miss the sting of this pesky heel fly. However, the heel fly was coming with such speed and force that it struck the tree with a bang, driving the sting into the tree. The heel fly was dead, but his sting worked right on through the tree, coming out on the opposite side. It fell to the ground, and wiggled along, plowing the earth with a furrow six inches deep and no less than eight inches wide until it had gone ten or twelve feet from the tree. There it died.

Moreover, the dogie was bound hard and fast by the loops and curves of the earthworm. The field lark, being frightened by so sudden an interruption, had let go of the worm and flown away. When the lark turned the worm loose, it bounded back like a powerful wire spring, curling and twining itself hard and fast around the dogie's four legs, causing it to fall.

Ab Jones, rounding up the straying dogies, found this one tied securely to the earthworm. When he looked at the spectacle, his first thought was that cattle thieves were branding dogies, and he actually searched for the fire, and the branding equipment. But upon further examination, his thoughts changed. He knew at once what had happened. He himself had been chased once by a heel fly, but had outwitted it by falling flat on the ground and letting it whiz past him in the pasture until it found a more interesting prospect.

He was very sorry, however, that the tree was stung, for now it had a large brown spot on each side of its trunk that would look like a big round target made by some inept marksman trying out a new kind of arrow. Moreover, the whole tree might die.

There on the ground before Ab lay the dogie, bawling and struggling helplessly in the throes of a powerful earthworm. But he thought, "Shucks!" This earthworm was not quite as large as one he had seen previously. However, the previous one was only the shell of a dead earthworm, with water pouring swiftly through it from the side of a steep bluff just after a heavy rain. It reminded him of a large, broken water main.

What had slipped Ab's memory, however, was the time a huge earthworm had worked his way through the bottom of a high railroad embankment not far from his home, and left a big tunnel underneath it. The water from a ten-inch rainfall had surged through this tunnel, undermining the tracks for a half mile or more, and had almost caused a major train wreck.

After his hurried investigation, Ab loosed the little unlucky dogie from the throes of the earthworm, and it ran away through the bushes, limping and bellowing.

The earthworm was none the worse for the experience, although it had lost one of its gizzards in the affray.

Ab spoke about having the heel fly mounted to show future generations the cause of the abrasions on the great oak, if it happened to live, but he decided it might not be practical, after all. Anyway, heel flies were a common thing, and so were big oak trees.

Raising Plenty Sand

ABE LUNKINS LIVED over in a section of the country known as the "Sand Hills." The soil in these sand hills was so poor that scarcely anything could live there. Ab Jones, a native of a nearby community, declared he had found a jack rabbit going across this section of the country carrying a *morral* over its head, eating oats as it

WALTER McKINNEY

went along to keep from starving. Old man Huggins, another native, said he could verify the statement.

"Why, it's so pore the red ants have turned pale pink, and grass burrs and seeds are so scarce that the ants have seedless days so's they won't starve to death."

Mr. Simpson, a third native, said that really the sand was so poor you would have to fertilize it to make good cement. Chookums Purdy said that he knowed it wuz so cause he ketched a half dozen gophers er mo' with coco grass nut roots in their pockets carrying them along as they traveled through the sandhills.

Now, Abe Lunkins had vowed that he "waren't never gonna work." He'd "just make the sand frum them ar' hills buy his meat an' bread."

But Mrs. Simpson, who lived fifty miles away in another community, scoffed, "Who would think about sand paying fer anything? Sand is common. Most everyone in our community has a small patch of sand on his place some'rs. In fact, they have to have sand to raise good sweet 'taters."

It was generally known, over several neighborhoods, that Abe Lunkins was a good-for-nothing parasite on the public. Sometimes when he got a "smart spell" on himself, and that was not often, he would have his wife and six children saw down a couple of post oak or blackjack trees. They would cut and stack the wood in a neat pile somewhat the shape of a wigwam. Abe would set fire to it then, and his children had to cover it over with dry sand. The fire would smoulder for a week or more, and make charcoal. His wife and children then dug it out, bagged it, and carried it to town in their old buckboard, and peddled it out to customers. The "revenooers," as the natives called the government agents, kept a close watch up in that direction at all times for stills, especially where there was smoke. But shucks! Abe was always too lazy to raise the grain even if he knew how to run a still. Which he probably didn't.

Since spring was coming on, Abe did not get any more of these smart spells on himself. He lay around in the shade and slept most of the time. His wife and children did what work they could find to do in the neighborhood so they could buy a sack of corn meal and some salt pork once in a while.

More recently, though, Abe began to "spruce up," for some reason. His wife looked better, and so did his children. Their close neighbors were wondering where he had got the money. It was good money, too.

Now, people living forty or fifty miles away were feeling the effects of a dreadful sandstorm, which seemingly had started in the hills. The sand settled on everything. No house could be kept free of sand. No wash on the line was clean. In fact, no one seemed clean. People went about all day grating sand between their teeth. Some were annoyed, and some took it as a matter of course. Some laughed and said that even the babies in the community were cutting their teeth on sand.

"Well, folks hafta' eat a peck o' sand anyway sometime in their life, so they mout as well eat it now," laughed the elder Mrs. Jones.

Once, during one of the worst sandstorms ever known, Ab Jones and Old Man Huggins went armadillo hunting up in the Sand Hills. They could not work anyhow during the storms, and armadillo meat, they thought, was good to eat. When they arrived up there, they were amazed to find themselves right in the spot where the sandstorms began. Suddenly, they heard a loud noise, something like a dog snapping its teeth together, but greatly magnified. The noise seemed to come from all directions. They first thought it was a mad bobcat, but one mad bobcat could not be in all directions making the same very loud noise. They listened and then began to look about them. Even their horses became restive.

They saw some very strange animals walking around that somehow reminded them of mangy, half-grown shoats. Still, these animals had long, flat, broad tusks resembling those of elephants, only they curved over their heads more and were eight to ten feet long. These broad tusks projected from strong jaws. Furthermore, these funny animals had peculiarly shaped heads, and were raising plenty of sand. Their jaws snapped loudly each time they dived their tusks into the sand, and threw it quickly into the air. The sand was thrown up no less than three hundred and fifty feet. On further examination, Ab and Old Man Huggins found this to be a colony of monstrous doodle bugs.

The doodle bugs had made a discovery. Each night, an army of cutting ants passed that way going to the newly-leafed post oak trees. These cutting ants were as large as house cats, and not only did they cut leaves, but whole branches of the trees, which they carried along. If Shake-speare's old Macbeth had been there at this time, he would have been horrified anew to see an entire forest once more on the move.

Now, the doodle bugs were digging funnel-shaped traps to catch the cutting ants on their nocturnal journeys. From all appearances, some of these doodle bugs certainly had made very good catches. However, their digging caused terrible duststorms; the fine sand being thrown high was carried away by the wind. But the coarse sand lay in great white heaps like piles of sugar. The best machinery could not have cleaned the sticks, leaves, and other debris and trash from the sand so thoroughly.

Now, about seventy-five miles away, a big highway was being built; sand was needed. Mrs. Lunkins heard of this, and drove to the office of the Highway Department. She made a trade with the Department to sell them sand for fifteen cents per load. It was not long before the Lunkins' neighbors began to wonder where this sudden affluence came from, especially, after Mrs. Lunkins had shown some of them her new cookstove, the first she had got since her marriage to Abe.

When the highway workmen arrived in the hills, they, too, were amazed. But they had sand to haul and could not waste time on trifles. Some of them might have been a little "skittish" of the doodle bugs at first, but, of course, they would not dare admit such a thing. However, one workman was heard to say that he could have used a good .22 gun if he had one, as "he had seen a stray squirrel on the road up there." But his fellow workmen winked at each other and shook their heads naively.

Now, the Highway Department employees, being kindly disposed men, were at first perplexed as to what to do with the doodle bugs while they loaded sand each day, and some thought that their trucks would be such a hazard to these harmless creatures that they felt like abandoning the job. But the foreman was called out to look over the situation and he soon had a plan satisfactory to all. The Highway Department was to build large pens of chicken wire (and they actually did) to corral the doodle bugs. The back sides of these pens were camouflaged so as to appear to be great piles of sand. Each morning, the doodle bugs were herded into these enclosures for the day, and were turned loose at night. The doodle bugs were not hard to round up, as some of the highway workmen had lived on farms and knew how to drive hogs. When the doodle bugs were driven to the wide gates and saw what they presumed to be great piles of dirt, they nearly knocked down the gates backing to the camouflaged pyramids of sand. After this daily routine was put into practice, the road workers came with their trucks and loaded sand with no interruptions.

Nevertheless, there was one hazard to the workmen. The doodle bugs had made their funnel-shaped traps so deep that if a workman fell into one, he needed a ladder to climb out. So everyone had to be careful and carry a small ladder on each truck.

The doodle bugs, being let out of their pens at night, worked fiercely to build their traps again for the cutting ants. Hence, the duststorms were worse at night. During the day, however, doodle bugs were industriously raising sand over in another pasture where the road workers were not loading it.

Now, some of the highway men, while loading their trucks with the sand, had, at times, to remove the carcasses of cutting ants. But that did not happen very often.

These workers were not bothered so much with the sand-storms as they were with one other thing. They carried their drinking water on a truck in a great container resembling a half tin cistern. It must have held four thousand gallons of water. One day when the noon signal was about to be given, a loud noise was heard. It sounded something like a very thirsty person at a cold drink stand sucking out the last bit of Coke from his glass, only it sounded ten times as loud. Everyone looked toward the water tank in time to see an extremely large mosquito in the act of flying away. It had sipped out their last drop of water from a tank that was more than two-thirds full! Away it flew, whirring its wings like the wheel of a giant plane. After this, old Uncle Dan, a colored workman now almost ready to be retired, consented to guard the water tank if he were allowed to carry a machine gun, and take a nap at noon each day.

Then the loading of sand continued without a ripple. Some of the doodle bugs became pets, and seemed very tame.

The foreman of the Highway Department thought of carrying one of the doodle bugs home and making a pet of it for his children, but he decided against it because he did not want it raising sand in his potato patch.

Ab Jones and Old Man Huggins deferred their hunting trip after they had found several armadillo shells lying about with a doodle bug tusk or so through them. They knew just what had happened. The armadillos had lost the fight and had moved to safer territory.

Some of the people in Jones' community threatened (and they had blood in their eye, too) to get out an injunction against the perpetrators of the duststorms, but they just never did. Anyhow, who knew anything about an injunction — especially a doodle bug?

Two Irishmen Walk

MR. DOOLEY, who hauled groceries
in his big truck each week for the
Neighborhood General Store, had
brought Patrick Sullivan and
Michael Kelly out from town. He had
put them off on Bruce Lane to walk the
rest of the way from the main road
to the back entrance of the
Bruce Ranch. The
foreman of the ranch,
Mr. Blank, had asked
him to bring them
out, as this was
a very busy time during
branding season and
all the cow hands were
working hard.

Pat and Mike had arrived from New York in the little town of Ranchine the evening before. They had saved money for several years so they could come to the Southwest and work on a ranch. From Bruce Lane, it was several miles to the ranch home known as The Big White House. These Irishmen had a cowboy friend, Aryle Crotty, working on the ranch. Aryle had written them such astounding stories about ranch life that they were eager to become ranch hands.

Pat and Mike had been in "Americky" about fifteen years, living in the city, and they were still as green as Erin itself when it came to ranch life. Sure, they had herds and pastures back in the old country, but not ranches of four or five thousand acres where a man might become lost. This was simply unimaginable to them.

It was not quite daylight when Mr. Dooley put Pat and Mike out in the lane. He always left home at four o'clock, on the mornings when he hauled groceries. He wanted to get back home quickly and finish some plowing. It was a spring morning, and the fog was very thick.

Following directions given them, the Irishmen walked down the lane and had gone up and down a couple of hills. This part of the country had a hill scattered about here and there. On the side of the next hill, now almost in view, the old cemetery was located. There was only a dirt road leading to this graveyard. Therefore, on rainy days it was hard to hold burials there. Since it was just about filled, the Cemetery Ladies' Associaton had decided to abandon it and find a better place.

As Pat and Mike neared this place, they were first awed and then astounded. Close to the road in the cemetery, they saw what to them looked like a whitish-colored cow lying under the burden of an enormous gravestone. It seemed that this stone had fallen on the cow. However, this grave marker was oddly shaped; it resembled a toy top which is spun with a string. It was turned upside down.

"Holy smoke! We must take the tombstone off th' critter! She will die!" cried Mike as they climbed the fence to aid the cow.

"Mother of saints!" cried Pat. "This beast has no hair on it, and look at its horns! Why, just feel of them! They are soft like its skin. This is a new kind of cow. Look! Look! Its horns are folding in! That must be something new — a folding cow! Maybe it is one of those vest pocket affairs I have read about. Americans are so resourceful. They think of everything." continued Pat.

"By all the Saints in Erin! Its horns are coming out again, and it is moving! Why, it is taking the tombstone along with it," cried Mike.

"That's not a cow. It is some critter born of the divil to stay around this graveyard. Let's get away from here," observed Pat.

"It has no legs, but feet hooked onto its body. Look at it move! This road back of it looks like someone has been paving it," said Mike as they returned to the road.

About that time, Pat, filled with excitement and not watching where he walked, slipped down and went sliding to the foot of the hill so fast he hardly knew what had happened. Mike was lucky enough to jump to the side of the road when he saw how slippery it was.

This strange animal was only a huge snail as large as a giant steer. On that foggy morning, he was out, as usual, crawling. He had crawled up the road leaving a trail of slime behind him, as all snails do, and had gone into the cemetery. Pat's trousers and hands were not only dirty with slimy mud, but he was as angry as any red-headed, freckle-faced Irishman can possibly get.

At the bottom of the hill was a small creek. When it

rained, the creek became five or ten feet deep where vehicles crossed, but a few feet above this crossing there were stepping-stones where pedestrians could cross at all times. Pat and Mike were in a dilemma when they first saw the creek ahead. Mr. Dooley had forgotten to mention the creek to them. However, when they came to the water's edge, they saw that there was a peculiar bridge over the creek. At least, it was mysterious to Pat and Mike. This strange bridge glistened, looked scaly at the opposite end, and was fan-shaped at the entrance. The moment they stepped on this bridge, it moved. When they had taken several steps further, something happened suddenly! They never knew just what! They found themselves in the air for a moment, then safely on the other side of the creek, sitting in the sand. They looked around just in time to see an enormous perch swim away; it had been basking in the foggy, balmy air on top of the water. It had been just lying on its side resting while partially asleep. Only its tail and a little of its body was showing when Pat and Mike arrived on the scene. They thought it was a bridge and stepped aboard, only to be flipped over to the other side.

One of the colored people in the community had been telling the story of seeing a huge perch in the deeper parts of the creek, but colored folk had had optical illusions before. Other colored folk, however, said they had seen an enormous eye as large as a dinner plate among some driftwood in that creek after a big rain. They said it looked so long at them, never blinking, that the creek was condemned by all the colored people as being haunted. None of them wished to see an unblinking eye staring at them; so the creek was said to have an evil eye, or "hants" in the water. Slim Johnson, a colored vagrant, declared that he had seen this eye, but it had blinked at *him*. However, his story was not given much credence, since he had never been held in very high regard by his people. Nevertheless, some of the church people declared that the evil eye had blinked at "dat niggah caze he wuz sich a chicken thief." So went the story over the neighborhood.

Pat walked over to the edge of the creek and washed as much slime and mud off as he could, before they continued their journey on down the road. Down the lane, only a short distance away, was a big gate. Pat and Mike walked through the gate as they had been directed to do by Mr. Dooley, and started down the wide dirt road which led through the pasture to the ranch house. They noticed a sign along the road which read, "Bird Reserve, No Shooting Allowed." They had not gone far when they heard a chopping, or hacking, sound. Yet it seemed to be neither. They had heard people chop wood in a forest before; that was nothing new. However, as they neared the scene of chopping, the air was full of wood dust, very fine sawdust, and small chips mixed with coarse sawdust flying in every direction. Pat and Mike were anxious to meet some of the ranch people so they walked toward the sound of the chopping. The air was so thick they could hardly see where they were going. And they found there were no woodsmen at all! There were only two giant woodpeckers building a nest in an enormous old hickory nut tree.

"Did ye iver see the likes o' this?" murmured Pat to Mike as they watched silently.

"I niver," replied Mike.

"Let's be laving," said Pat, as he brushed some chips from his shoulders.

"By all the Saints, Oi am verra' sure this is a quare kentry," cried Mike.

Just as they were entering the road once more, Pat said, "By faith, and what's that moving behind the log out there?"

"And where might that be?" asked Mike. But he had already seen something bobbing up and down behind a great old oak log.

Pat, leaving Mike behind, hurried over to see this unusual sight, hiding behind the trunk of a nearby tree. A yellow and black tarantula spider, weighing seventy-five to one hundred and fifty pounds, was moving slowly along by the log. It was closing in on a big possum, which was absolutely unaware of any danger. The possum was busily engaged eating small blackberries which grew under the protecting shelter of this old log. Pat's eyes almost popped out of his head. when he saw the possum.

"B'gorra, an' sure that's the biggest wood rat in the wurrld," he said in a whisper to himself.

About that time he felt something pat him lightly on the shoulder. His judgment clouded by amazement, Pat thought Mike was by his side watching the same spectacle and only patting his friend in a silent comment of wonder. But when he turned around, he froze in his tracks, horrified. His "pats" had been coming from the legs of another huge tarantula that was climbing up the tree, from behind which Pat had been peeping. The spider was trying to use him as a step in climbing the tree. Pat jumped from back of the tree, and hurried in the direction of the road, too scared to utter a sound.

Mike had seen a plot of bluebonnets at the other side of the road, and was down on his knees picking some when Pat joined him.

"The divil is staking all his cohorts in this place! B'gorra, let's be 'auf," said Pat breathlessly.

Mike said nothing but just raised a bunch of bluebonnets up for his friend's approval.

"We should soon be there for breakfast. Sure, and some coffee would taste mighty foine," said Pat, taking a deep breath. They started off. The fog had lifted a little. A noise like a playful puppy was heard by both Irishmen. Before they knew it, they had walked up on a tearful little colored boy sitting by the road. He had a couple of large lumps on his head. By his side were three unbelievably huge feathers, resembling in size some two-by-four pieces of lumber. Each was at least six feet long. They were just some plumage from a mockingbird which had had a fight with a woodpecker in the top of the old oak. The woodpecker seemed to have won, from the looks of things. However, the woodpecker had not left the field of battle unscathed, as there were some small red feathers about the size of a man's hand still floating about in the air.

The little boy was Moses, the ranch cook's nephew.

"I wuz pickin' berries under dat tree," he told them, pointing to an enormous tree, "we'n dese fedders fell outen de tree an' hit me on de haid. I'se afeerd to go git de buckets ob berries by de tree, now," said the little colored boy. The Irishmen looked in wonder. Meantime, over to one side, a fat little yellow mongrel pup was playing around a large black cricket, no less then the size of a grown duck. The puppy would run up to the cricket to catch it in his mouth, then the cricket would hop over him ten or fifteen feet away. Then the pup would circle around it, barking and growling.

On seeing that the Irishmen were not cow hands but strangers, and because little Moses knew all the ranch people, he said, "Who is yo' all?"

"We are Patrick Kelley and Michael Sullivan," said Mike.

"We hev' coom' to the r-r-ranch to be coo'hands, B'faith. An' can you tell us wher-r to go?"

"Yassuh," said Moses, wiping the tears from his eyes. "Come heah, yo' Yaller Hammer, an' leav' dat cricket 'lone.

I don' tole yo' oncet about dat cricket. Youse gwin' to cause us all bad luck a botherin' it. We's gwine ter sho' dese gemmen de big white house now." And with these words, Moses started to lead the way.

Mike, feeling sorry about the bumps on the little colored boy's head, went over to the tree and picked up the buckets. They were almost full of delicious blackberries.

With the berries safe by his side, little Moses forgot his crying and directed the Irishmen to the place where many strange adventures awaited them.

Wonder Valley

SITUATED BETWEEN two hills lay a broad, rich valley. However, the hills were scarcely noticeable as there was so much land between them.

The trees in this valley, mostly pecans, were very

large and very productive. The farm crops too were large
each year, and many strange things happened here. Nevertheless, the people around "these parts" seemed very happy
and contented.

Now, for instance, the Bixby family lived on a tract of
land in the center of the valley. But Old Man Bixby always
leased forty or fifty acres on "The Rim" for his cabbage
patch. The Rim was a stretch of land lying along the outside of Wonder Valley, not far from the Bruce Ranch. Many
farmers leased land on the rim for their cabbage crops.

Mr. Bixby had several hundred acres in his own tract,
but could not raise cabbage there. The community around
him just would not allow it! So he had to lease land outside
somewhere.

The cabbages made so much noise growing that the
natives were disturbed in their peaceful slumbers. This one
vegetable seemed to grow mostly during darkness. The loud
slap, slap, slap of each leaf cupping itself around the other
leaves as the heads were formed and the rip, rip, rip of the
roots spreading out in the soil, would have awakened the
dead. Then, occasionally, there was a loud pow-wow or bang,
bang! Some of the cabbages just exploded, they were growing so fast.

But shucks! Those who owned the land around about
seemed to have calluses on their eardrums, including some
folks of Wonder Valley. For during pecan picking season,
did not the whole community hire Zeke Moody to get the
pecans off the trees? Now, Zeke was a very unusual person.
He had great nasal power. He lived about two "wagon
greasings" away from this community, but he was never forgotten during pecan picking season.

All that each pecan tree owner did was to place a tem-
porary fence of hog wire around the trees to keep away the
neighborhood hogs — and Zeke did the rest. He brought his

tent and a cot and spent the night under one group of four or five trees at a time. He snored so loud that the trees were violently shaken for fifty yards around, and the pecans were piled on the ground so high by morning that Zeke sometimes had to dig his way out. Now, he usually slept under a pup tent, but the pecans hit his bunions sometimes, which cut down the power of his snoring. So he had to place a smaller tent over his feet. When morning came, Zeke moved his tents to the next grove of pecan trees. Someone else had to pick them up; Zeke only surveyed his work to see if his snores might be lacking in power, then satisfied, moved on.

This year, during his snores, the puffs of wind from both nostrils and mouth blew the tops off of Lum Stubbins' small haystacks nearby. Lum just had not had time to gather all his second hay crop into his barns. However, he knew what might happen to it, in that particular hay meadow during pecan picking season.

One of the smart alecs of the neighborhood, Ginks Mulligan, during the night placed a portable windmill, with a cistern, where it would get the full blasts of Zeke's puffs. He rigged it up with pipes running to a nearby creek. The windmill pumped so much water during the night that the portable cistern ran over and flooded the place where Zeke was sleeping.

The thing about it which hacked Zeke so much was that the next morning he was still sound asleep, and his cot was floating about in a pool of water. Several squirrels that had rescued themselves from the flood were sharing his bed and eating nuts.

The people who lived near the pecan trees said they did not know which made the worst noise, Zeke's snoring or the squealing pigs running back and forth around the fence trying to get into where Zeke was sleeping. They knew from previous experience that pecans were being harvested. The people in the neighborhood said also that they could not possibly stand the noise more than once a year.

Old Man Hilburn, who lived on "The Rim," had bought a couple of those pigs to fatten before hog killing season, which was just around the corner. Now, the old man was no light snorer himself. He said that these "confounded pigs" heard him snoring and squealed so loud at night that he had to move their pen a distance of six hundred "ax-handles" away from his house because his wife, Betsy, could not sleep.

Now, Old Man Teller, another native of Wonder Valley, had some of the finest pecans in the neighborhood. They grew on a particular "pet tree" of his. He had worked for years with this tree. His father and grandfather had worked with it, putting all sorts of secret fertilizer about it, usually after dark. None of the neighbors could ever get him to divulge his secret fertilizer formula.

A small tent show had come to Wonder Valley for several days' showing. They had a cage of five or six trained monkeys. Ginks Mulligan thought it would be a funny joke to open the cage on the night of the last performance. However, the monkeys, instead of pestering the housewives of the community, as Ginks expected, went to the nearest pecan trees. Of course, these belonged to old man Teller.

The pecans on the pet tree were so large that the monkeys presumed them to be small coconuts. So the next morning when the monkeys were found, all but one, that is, they were having a lot of fun chunking each other with pecans. Mr. Teller offered a reward of $50 to anyone with knowledge of how the monkeys escaped. No one claimed it. The missing monkey had gone to young Mrs. Briley's yard and had got into her baby's buggy. Mrs. Briley had put her baby out into the sun in its buggy early that morning, but luckily she had just taken it into the house to feed it. However, she had left the buggy out in the yard. She intended to bring the baby back for more early morning sunshine. This monkey had snugly covered himself up, with only his head and face visible. Grandma Voss, who was walking along the road, saw the buggy and stopped to admire the baby. Her vision was very bad.

"If that youngun' ain't the spittin' image of its old gramp, Hoolihan, whiskers an' all! I intend to tell the ole coot so, the very next time I see him. I know he'll be pleased," she said as she walked slowly back to the road.

The show people were rather embarrassed. All the neighborhood had one more try at catching the monkeys. This theatrical group was delayed a whole day and night from their next show place, which was about three "wagon greasings" away.

But back to Zeke: He was staying away from the men now who gathered at the neighborhood store, especially on Saturday afternoons. His wife could not even get him to go over and get the mail there.

Some of these men who collected at the store were Old Trail Drivers, who talked and exchanged their stories of driving up The Trail. Sometimes, they tried to surpass each other in tall tales. Many tales were told, but two were prize winners. Uncle Ted Coulter and Uncle Si Brown had told them. Uncle Ted told this story:

While he was riding slowly along on horseback one afternoon, away from his herd, he was confronted suddenly with a greyhound chasing a jack rabbit. Neither seemed to see Uncle Ted and his horse. They came headlong toward him and his mount. He ducked quickly, only to have his horse and himself cleared in a jump by the jack rabbit. But the greyhound just jumped through the left stirrup of his saddle without even touching it!

Uncle Si Brown told this one which was also about a jack rabbit. He said he was out hunting late one afternoon up

The Trail, when he happened upon a strange phenomenon. He found a common old hound dog with his neck locked tightly in the forepaws of a jack rabbit. Both had just died! The rabbit had died of sheer exhaustion and the hound had died of utter shame!

The storekeeper had placed some boxes and empty barrels out on the store porch to accommodate the men of the neighborhood. This was the third group of barrels and boxes to be placed there in the last several years. They had all been whittled to pieces by the neighborhood men who collected at the store on Saturdays. That is, all except one barrel, and Old Man Halloran, who weighed something like six hundred and seventy-five pounds, had simply squashed that one. It was a molasses barrel which everyone thought could hold the weight of a ton. Old man Halloran always sat on that particular barrel on Saturdays. That was the only time he came to the store. He did not like it if anyone beat him to this barrel. Several people over the community said they would almost be willing to swear in any court that Ginks Mulligan, the aforementioned smart alec, and his gang had "altered" that barrel one night because the barrel "broke up" in mighty "peculiar pieces" as Old Man Halloran sat on it. After it happened, most of the men found they had some very important business inside the store or at home, and left the porch.

Two of the men, it was reported, simply killed the grass so dead in one spot on the roadside home where they had laughed and rolled on it that it took two years for the grass to grow out again.

Zeke had been holding the men on the store porch spellbound for a couple of Saturdays, with some of his yarns. Some of the men had dubbed him with the name of "Old Continued Story." One story he related was that a strange thing had happened to his grandson, Buddy Perkins, who was only seven years old, over in Badman's Pool. The story went like this:

It seems that Buddy and his dog, old Rip, had wandered down to this pool. People seldom came here, as it was supposed to have "hants" on it. The legend about this pool was that a long time ago some thugs had murdered and robbed an old Dutchman there. Some of the natives had seen, as they thought, the murder and robbery re-enacted late in the evening there, and strange noises were heard around about the pool at dusk many times since then. So this place was seldom visited.

Buddy and old Rip were chasing frogs when Rip discovered a big soft shell turtle. He started barking furiously at the turtle, when a monstrous perch swam to the water's edge, slid onto the mud and green moss, and blew water into old Rip's face. Rip thought the fish was playing, so he jumped about the fish, barking loudly.

The perch stood his ground, and came closer to old Rip. It finned him on his face, making a wound four or five inches long. Rip then began to growl. When Buddy, who was ramming a stick in a crawfish hole close by, heard the growl, he knew there must be danger near. So he took his dog and ran home.

Buddy told his parents about the fish and showed them the cut on Rip's face. At first, his parents did not believe him and threatened to give him "a whaling in the woodshed" for outright lying. But when Buddy stuck to his story, they became astonished and his father vowed he would go to the pool the very next morning, and try to catch the perch.

Next day, he went rabbit hunting and stopped by the pool "just for fun." He had his lunch and a canteen of water so he could browse around all day if he chose. His wife had painted the canteen a bright red color, so if "John lost it, as he has lost two others, maybe he will find it this time."

When John came to the pool, it was very calm. There was not a ripple nor a bubble on it. Everything about it spoke of sleep. He pulled off his shoes, rolled up his trousers, and waded into the pool. He suddenly stepped off into a deep hole which seemed to have an undercurrent; but since he was a good swimmer, he soon swam out. However, he had lost his canteen; the strap simply came off his shoulders while he was swimming.

He swam back to shallow water and waded out. He sat for a while on the banks thinking about his experience, and was trying to dry his wet clothing when a monstrous perch came sliding into the shallow water. John was so amazed at the sight that he just gaped at first. Suddenly, he saw a red strap hanging from the mouth of the perch.

"My canteen strap! He swallowed up my canteen!" John yelled loudly.

"That feller's got my canteen! Reckon I can git 'em an' th' canteen too. All my neighbors could have fish then!" he said to himself.

He ran to this daring fish, caught him by two of his fins and tried to pull him to the banks; but the perch finned John badly on his arms and would not budge an inch. John then tried to drag the fish out by pulling on the canteen strap. He wrapped the strap around his wrists and pulled hard, but the perch could not be moved. By this time, John was bleeding profusely. The fish backed out of the mud, and pulled the man with him into the deep water. Now John had to let go of the canteen strap, because the perch was pulling him underwater.

Zeke first told this story to a group of men on the store porch one Saturday afternoon. At first, the men listened, as he was always telling some miraculous yarn; but later, they told him that the wounds on John's arms and limbs were probably caused from trouble with John's mother-in-law, old Mrs. Harper.

Everyone in the neighborhood knew she was an old catamount, (most not knowing what the word meant). It was a new word the community smart alec had brought home with him from his one term in college.

After this story, when Zeke rode his horse up to the hitching posts, near the store porch, he would hear a loud guffaw, or a muffled chuckle, and see some of the men just grinning. So he shied away from the store porch now, especially on Saturdays. The men teased him too much about his fish story.

Speaking of Mrs. Harper as an old catamount, Mrs. Huggins of the same neighborhood said that the old lady had a perfect right to be that and then some.

"Did not five of her eight daughters marry good fer nuthin' men? Certainly! Lum Harkins married one, and Lum was just a 'sooner.' He had sooner sit down than work."

Mrs. Huggins said that she believed those neighborhood play parties where they "danced Josie," played "Goin' to Boston," "Skip to My Lou," and "Shoot the Buffalo" were "jist matchmakin' games."

"Yes, they wuz good behavior at thim ar' parties, but the boys who cu'd sing the loudes' wer' the good fer nuthin'st. Yep! That's whar' Lum got his wife."

Now, Lum and his family were the talk of the neighborhood. They had thirteen kids, two hound dogs, a couple of pigs, and an old milk goat. They all shared the same shack. There was a "youngun" that slept at the foot of each bed, and a whole herd slept on two of granny's old trundle beds. The whole neighborhood said that "they just knowed thet Lum junior was a dwarf because he had always slept at the foot of the bed when he was little."

The Harkins family had a garden patch right by the house. In this garden, one thing grew for certain and that was a sweet potato vine. The agricultural agent had asked Lum and his wife one time if this vine were a perennial, but both spoke up at once and said, "No, it's a 'tater vine."

All the other vegetables, such as turnips, beets, collards, beans, onions, and mustard died out during summer or were eaten up, but this potato vine still thrived each year. It usually had two potatoes on it. One was a large potato, the other a small one.

When the neighbors passed by the place, they always looked at the house. In fact, this house was the thermometer of the community. If the house was reared up on the south side, the whole neighborhood knew about it, and the remark was made that winter was just around the corner "because Lum Harkin's house was up on one side." When the foundation settled back to normal in the spring, then word went over the neighborhood again. But this time, it was to announce that "winter was over" now for sure!

It happened this way: One of the potatoes grew so large that it raised the whole foundation of the house on the south side! All the family and animals (including a few rats) ate on this potato all winter. Lum just built a cornstalk and dirt potato kiln up to the side of the house over the vine, after the first frost. By the time winter was over, the foundation of the house was back to normal, for the potato was about eaten up. This happened year after year. He placed the smaller potato on a truck with a block and tackle and carried it to his mother each year.

The neighborhood always used this house raising and lowering to announce winter and spring. In the spring, off came the red flannels, and in the fall, on they went.

One time though, the whole neighborhood was fooled.

The rats were so large in the community that they carried Lum's old jackscrew down into the kiln and used it under the foundation for a listening post!

Fishie! Fishie!

HIRAM NUCKLEHEAD had been trying for six months to catch a certain bass in a near-by lake. He had utterly failed! He was actually asham-ed because Grandpap Nuckle-head had always been a good fisherman, and even boasted about it. Hiram just did not want to let the family name

down, where catching fish was concerned.

He devised an ingenious method that might fool the very biggest bass in any lake. He bought some extra powerful loadstone. He cut this loadstone in chunks, each about the size of a baseball. Now he disguised each piece with brightly colored flies. Then he rowed across the lake, dropping these chunks, mostly in the middle of the lake where he thought "Mr. Bass" might be hiding. As soon as these brightly colored pieces of loadstone hit the water, the bass swallowed them! Hiram had never seen so many bass!

"I'll show this community that even a mere mention of the name Nucklehead means big bass fishing," he said, as he rowed back to the shore feeling rather smug.

"But now comes the test of the whole thing," said Hiram to himself, a few minutes later, when he started out again across the lake in a brand new boat with a thick tin bottom.

He had not rowed his boat very far toward the center of the lake when things started to happen.

"Clunk! Pong! Bing! Clug!" went the fish hitting, and sticking to the bottom of the boat. They stacked up so thick and fast on the tin part that the boat was lifted out of the water.

The fish kept coming, and the boat kept rising slowly out of the lake until Hiram could not reach the water with his oars. Finally, his boat rose no less than twenty feet above the water.

A flock of hungry pelicans flew over. They saw the fish and started filling their pouches, but each time a bass was put into a pouch, "Clunk" went the pelican to the side of the boat, sticking hard and fast. Finally, there were pelican heads stuck completely around the rim of the boat. There never was such clacking and chuckling of pelicans. And there never was such flopping of wings and scrambling of feet! Hiram was actually afraid that these birds would stretch their wings out in unison, and fly off with him in the boat.

The boat rocked several times, and Hiram declared that the pelicans did lift it up distinctly a few feet out of the water each time, with the column of bass still hanging to it.

"This boat looks just like them in the canals in Venice or Italy or some place. Now, where did I see them when I was with the Navy that time? They were real pretty," said Hiram as he started pulling off pelicans and dropping them into the water.

But shucks! As soon as he dropped each bird, the load-stone drew it right back to the boat.

Finally, Hiram was rescued late that night by a searching party, sent out from the Bruce Ranch by his wife.